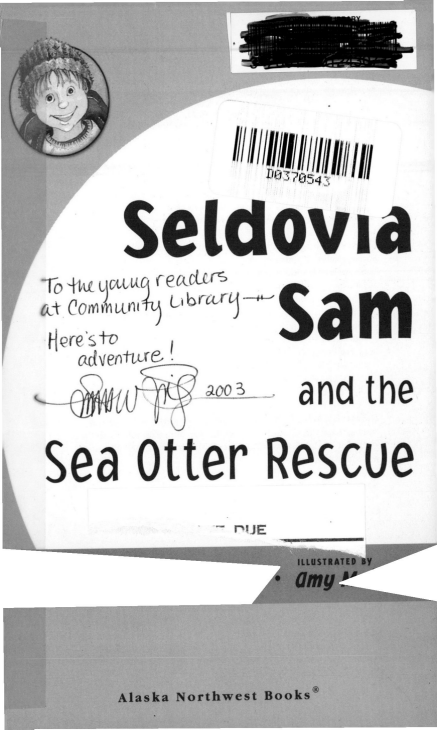

Seldovia

To the young readers
at Community Library—

Here's to
adventure!

2003

Sam

and the

Sea Otter Rescue

ILLUSTRATED BY
Amy M

Alaska Northwest Books®

To Olivia Meredith Butler. Read, Dream, Live!
— S. W. S.

For Patty Dempsey, a great Alaskan mom.
— A. C. M.

Text © 2003 by Susan Woodward Springer
Illustrations © 2003 by Amy Meissner

Library of Congress Cataloging-in-Publication Data
Springer, Susan Woodward.
    Seldovia Sam and the sea otter rescue / written by
Susan Woodward Springer ; illustrated by Amy Meissner.
        p. cm. — (Seldovia Sam ; 2)
Summary: Sam rescues and cares for an abandoned baby sea otter until it can be taken to a zoo.
    ISBN 0-88240-577-2
    [1. Sea otter—Fiction. 2. Animals—Infancy—Fiction. 3. Wildlife rescue—Fiction.] I. Meissner, Amy, ill. II. Title. III. Series.
    PZ7.S768465 Sd 2003
    [E]—dc21   2002010731

The Alaska Zoo has been a popular home to injured, orphaned, and endangered arctic and subarctic animals for more than thirty years. It is located at 4731 O'Malley Road (Mile 2), Anchorage, AK 99507. See www.alaskazoo.org.

Alaska Northwest Books®
An imprint of Graphic Arts Center Publishing Company
P.O. Box 10306, Portland, Oregon 97296-0306
503-226-2402, www.gacpc.com

President: Charles M. Hopkins
Associate Publisher: Douglas A. Pfeiffer
Editorial Staff: Timothy W. Frew, Tricia Brown, Jean Andrews,
    Kathy Howard, Jean Bond-Slaughter
Production Staff: Richard L. Owsiany, Susan Dupere

Editor: Michelle McCann
Book and cover design: Andrea L. Boven / Boven Design Studio, Inc.

Printed in the United States of America

Contents

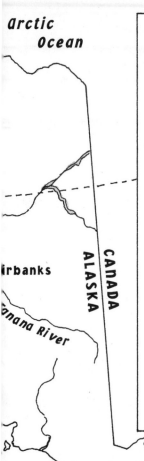

arctic
Ocean

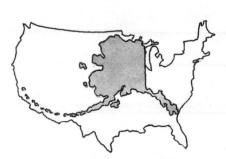

irbanks

anana River

CANADA
ALASKA

Alaska is so big that if you could lay it on top of the continental United States, it would cover one-fifth of all of the other states. And there really is a place called Seldovia. It's about 250 miles south of Anchorage. But there are no roads to get there. To reach Seldovia you have to fly in a plane or take a boat. Some of the place-names in Sam's stories are real; others are made up. Like Sam's parents, lots of men and women in Seldovia fly Bush planes and fish commercially. Is there a real Sam Peterson in Seldovia? Not by that name. But there's a little bit of Sam in all the kids in Seldovia, just as I suspect there's a little bit of Sam in you.

★ Juneau

Gulf of alaska

0   50   100   200 MILES

0   50   100   200 KILOMETERS

1

Hike to Sandy Cove

Sam and Neptune walked down the dirt road, past the fish cannery. Sam could hear the clinking of conveyor belts and the voices of the cannery workers. The heavy smell of fish floated on the foggy air, but Sam didn't mind. He was off to work on his fort at Sandy Cove.

Sam's driftwood fort promised to be a great place to spy on fishing boats as they chugged through the channel and out to sea. Today, Sandy Cove would be cold and wet, and most of the boats wouldn't dare to venture out in the fog where dangerous rocks would be hidden.

Sam passed the boatyard. Fishing boats sat up on wooden blocks, waiting for repairs and painting. Later in the day, the boatyard would be noisy with the whine of electric sanders, and busy men with ladders and buckets of paint. This morning, it was the *whaaaooo-whaaaooo* of the foghorn on the cliff that shattered the quiet.

Just past the boatyard, he came to the spruce forest and the trail that would take him to Sandy Cove. The trees were full of birds, all singing despite the rain.

Sam loved walking through the woods on the springy moss. Today it squished like a bright green sponge. Sam stepped carefully around the white flowers of dwarf dogwood and the tiny purple violets that poked through the moss. The sound of the foghorn grew softer as the trail left the village and wound along the coast.

Sam came to a mound of old clam and mussel shells left in the woods by ancient Indians who had feasted on them. He poked through the mound with a stick, hoping to find an arrowhead. "No arrowheads today, Neptune," he said, and continued on his way.

Next Sam passed the place where his mother came to gather wild mushrooms in the fall. He looked, but the mushrooms were still tiny spores, asleep under the moss. "No mushrooms today," said Sam.

Just ahead grew a thick stand of alder bushes. Sam stood at the edge of the alder patch and whistled and clapped his hands to scare away any black bears that might be feeding on the tender young grass. Out shot a squirrel. "Whew! No bears today," said Sam.

As they walked by a lagoon, Neptune startled a small flock of sea ducks. With a sudden flapping of wings, they took to the air. Neptune ran after them, barking. Sam chuckled, "No ducks today, Neptune."

The trail wound away from the lagoon and grew muddy. Sam hopped from log to log, and threw his arms to either side for balance. One more log, a patch of grass, and then . . . Sandy Cove!

It was so foggy that Sam couldn't see the red-and-green buoys in the water that marked the channel for the boats. The tide was low, and Sam could hear the waves breaking on the rock ledges, but he could barely make out their shapes.

Waaa-waaa.

Sam heard, or thought he heard, crying. He listened hard, but he didn't hear it again. Maybe it was just the foghorn at faraway Lookout Point. Sometimes, noises sounded strange in the fog . . .

2

A Voice in the Fog

Sam's fort was just as he left it, standing at the edge of the woods. Dad had helped Sam drag four big logs up the beach and arrange them in a square. Then Dad had cut long, straight alder branches and had driven them in the soft ground with a mallet. Dad had shown Sam how to nail driftwood boards to the alders, and how to brace the walls so they wouldn't fall in. The rest was up to Sam.

Every weekend since the snow had melted, Sam had come to Sandy Cove to scrounge for boards to build his walls.

Now all that was left to do was the roof. Sam couldn't wait to finish his fort so he and Neptune could spend the night there.

Waaa-waaa. Waaa-waaa.

There it was again. That faint crying sound.

Sam strained to listen, but all he heard was the *whisshhh-whisshh* of the gentle waves on the ledges.

"Come on. Let's go find some boards."

Sam and Neptune set off down the beach. In a jumbled pile of tree stumps and seaweed, Sam found three large silvery boards. They would be perfect for the roof! One by one, Sam dragged the boards back to his fort. They were very heavy, and it was hard work.

Sam sat down to rest for a moment, wiping sweat from his forehead.

Waaa-waaa.

There it was again, like a sad baby.

Neptune perked up her ears. She heard it too! Neptune ran down to the water and barked.

Aroof! Aroof!

Sam ran after her.

Waaa-waaa. Waaa-waaa.

It sounded as though it were coming from out on the water. Sam knew that sound traveled easily over water. Once, when he and Dad were on their fishing boat, anchored in a big bay, Sam heard voices. They sounded like they were on the boat, but when he came out on deck, Sam realized the voices were coming from

a boat anchored on the opposite shore!

Waaa-waaa.

A slight breeze scattered the fog for just a moment and Sam could see the rock ledges just off the beach. Something out there seemed to move.

Sam worked his way from rock to rock, moving closer to the ledges. Although the tide was low, a good stretch of water still lay between the ledges and the shore. It was too far to jump, and Sam couldn't tell how deep the water might be.

The little shape moved again and cried. It was a baby sea otter lying right on top of the rocks! Sam could just see its fuzzy head and bright round eyes. The fog began to lift in the breeze and Sam saw that the baby was alone. Sam knew that if the fog cleared and eagles spotted the defenseless baby, they would carry it off. He had to reach it . . . and soon!

The only way was through the water. Sam waded in. It was numbing cold but only went up to his knees. So far, so good.

Step . . . step . . . step . . . Sam moved out closer to the ledges. Maybe he could make it.

Step . . . step . . . Whooosh! Sam plunged into the water up to his neck! The cold knocked the breath out of his lungs and made his head ache!

Sam struggled back to shore and crawled out. He was a good swimmer, but the water was too cold. There was nothing to do but run back to the village to get help. Sam prayed the fog wouldn't clear before he could return to the baby otter.

3

A Cold, Wet Race against Time

Sam sprinted along the trail as fast as he could in his cold, wet, heavy clothes. He didn't hop from log to log, but sloshed right through the mud. He zipped past the lagoon, with Neptune at his heels. She didn't even stop to chase the ducks.

At the alder patch, Sam didn't stop to listen for bears, but ran on without thinking. He passed the mushroom patch and the Indian shell mound. He raced through the spongy moss. Sam was still running when he came to the dirt road.

He rounded the corner and spotted

Dad's red-and-white pickup truck at the boatyard. Dad was helping Hank Sutton paint the hull of his boat. Sam tore through the gate and skidded to a stop, gasping for breath. He and Neptune were soaking wet and covered with mud.

Between gulps of air, Sam managed to tell Dad about the baby sea otter. "He's abandoned, Dad. I heard him crying the whole time I was at Sandy Cove. The fog is lifting and I just know some old eagle is gonna see him and kill him if we don't get back there fast!

"Please, Dad. We can't let him die. You've got to come!" begged Sam.

Dad opened his mouth and looked as though he might be getting ready to say no, but Hank spoke up, "Take my motor scooter, Wally. That boy of yours doesn't look like he can run another step."

"All right, Sam," said Dad. "We'll see what

we can do. Thanks, Hank. We shouldn't be long."

Dad straddled the scooter and started the engine. Sam put Neptune into the bed of the pickup truck and told her to stay. He accepted a dry jacket from Hank and climbed on behind Dad. They putted off down the road.

Just as they reached the turnoff to the trail, Sam spotted Melody Chambers, know-it-all queen of Seldovia Elementary School.

Sam was glad she was too scared of bears to walk the trail to Sandy Beach. He didn't want anyone else to know about his discovery. As they sped by her, Sam tried to look like he went for scooter rides every day in soaking-wet clothes.

The scooter bounced over the trail, past the shell mound and the mushroom place, through the alder patch and past the lagoon.

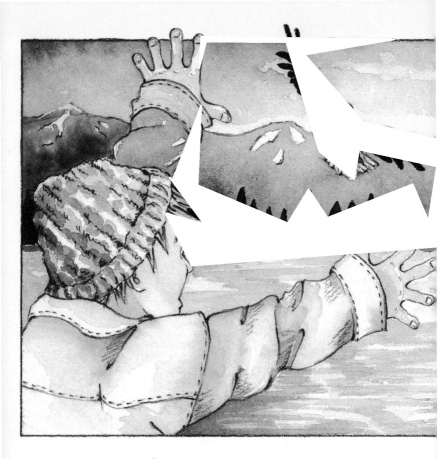

In no time, they were at Sandy Cove.

Just as Sam had feared, the fog was gone and three eagles were circling in the air above the baby otter! Sam sprinted toward the rocks, waving his arms in the air.

"Get away from there! Shoo!" he shouted.

The eagles were not leaving.

Waaa-waaa. Waaa-waaa, cried the little otter.

Dad caught up with Sam at the water's edge.

"Look, Sam. I'll try to get to him, but if those eagles snatch him first, there's nothing I can do. It's just nature taking its course.

You understand that, don't you, Sam?"

Sam nodded, but his eyes were fixed on the circling eagles. He didn't want nature to take its course this time.

"Hurry, Dad," he whispered, as the biggest eagle dropped lower in the sky, swooping closer and closer to the baby otter.

4

Sea Otter Rescue

Dad yanked off his leather boots, took a deep breath, and launched himself into the water with a giant belly flop. When he came up for air, he roared in surprise at the shock of the cold water.

It took Dad just a few strokes to swim across to the ledge, but it seemed like forever to Sam.

As Dad hauled himself out onto the rocks and stood up, the eagles scattered.

"Yeaaa, Dad!" cheered Sam, jumping up and down. "Way to go!"

Dad slowly approached the baby sea

otter. It was cold and tired and terrified. It didn't even try to get away. With one swift motion, Dad scooped it up and put it inside his coat. He zipped the coat up to his chin, turned and waded back into the water. Sam could hear Dad's teeth chattering as he drew near the shore.

On the beach, Dad unzipped his coat and handed the tiny bundle of fur to Sam. "You're drier than me, Sam. Put him in your jacket so he can stay warm."

Sam cuddled the baby otter. It had the softest fur he had ever felt—like velvet and very thick. It looked like a bundle of fur with two huge brown eyes peeking out. Sam put the otter next to his face. It smelled like fish, but fresh, not stinky.

Waaa-waaa. As the little baby cried, Sam saw its pink mouth with tiny sharp teeth, like a kitten's. Carefully, he tucked the otter in his jacket, and followed Dad up the beach to the scooter. The ride back to the village went quickly. Sam could feel Dad shivering as the cool air hit his wet clothes.

Dad left Sam at the boatyard and rode home to grab some dry clothes for them. Neptune jumped out of the truck and snuffled at the unfamiliar smell coming from Sam's jacket.

"Easy, girl," he laughed.

Hank and his helpers crowded around Sam, who opened his jacket just a bit. The baby otter squirmed and cried, *Waaa-waaa*.

"You know it's not legal to keep those critters," said a man in dirty overalls. "The Fish and Game guy will have to kill it if he can't find its mother."

"Don't upset the boy," scolded Hank.

How could anyone kill a poor, defense-less baby otter? thought Sam as he petted

its silky fur. *What did it ever do to anyone?*

"But, why . . . " he sputtered.

Just then Dad returned. "Come on, Sam. Let's take your baby over to the Fish and Game officer. Thanks for the scooter, Hank."

Oh no! They couldn't take the otter

there. Anywhere but there.

"Hey Dad, wait! We can't . . . "

But it was too late. Dad was already revving up the truck.

5

A Life-or-Death Decision

S am climbed in and they pulled out of the boatyard.

"Dad, we can't take the otter to the Fish and Game guy. He's gonna kill him!"

"Look, Sam," Dad said quietly, putting his hand on Sam's head, "We can't keep a wild animal as a pet. You have to let nature take its course."

Sam's eyes burned as he held back tears. Nature taking its course again—he didn't like it one bit. But he could tell that Dad had his mind made up. He would just have to think of a plan. And quick. They were already pulling up to the harbor building where the Fish and Game officer worked.

As they walked into the office, a large man in a khaki shirt and khaki pants turned to greet them.

"Afternoon, Walt," he said to Dad, shaking his hand. He tried to shake Sam's hand too, but Sam kept his hands tucked into his coat.

"Well," the officer said with a grin, "What can I do for you?"

Waaa-waaa, cried the squirming shape in Sam's coat, right on cue.

"What in the world have you got there?" asked the officer. Sam tried to cover the otter's mouth, completely forgetting those tiny sharp teeth.

"Ouch!" cried Sam as the baby otter nipped him.

"Show him, Sam," urged Dad.

Argh! Where was a plan when he needed one?

Very, very slowly, Sam unzipped his jacket. Out popped a fuzzy brown head. The otter's bright eyes blinked and he cried even louder, *Waaa-waaa.*

"Well, I'll be darned!" exclaimed the

officer. "That must be the baby that belongs to the dead female we found washed up on Stony Beach yesterday. Looked like something attacked her. Orca whale, maybe. Hard to say. We could tell she was nursing a pup, but there was no sign of him around. We figured the eagles got him."

"They almost did," burst Sam, "but my Dad swam out to the ledge and rescued him just in time!"

"Must've been a cold swim," chuckled the officer.

"It sure was," agreed Dad, "but . . . "

"You can't kill him," Sam interrupted. "He's just a baby. I won't let you do it!"

"Well, Sam," the officer said, as he cleared his throat and ran his fingers through his hair. "The problem is that he'll die anyway without his mother to feed and groom him. He's too little to fend for himself, and the law won't permit me to let you keep him as a pet."

Sam felt helpless before the Fish and Game officer, and his uniform, and his law. The officer's big muscular arms in the khaki shirt reached out to take the baby otter from him.

"Wait!" cried Sam, stumbling backwards, "I have an idea!"

6

Sam, the Sea Otter Mom

What about a zoo?" pleaded Sam. "The one in Anchorage has a sea otter pen. I've seen it!"

The officer sighed, "Last I heard they weren't taking any more sea otters."

Sam gave him a sour look.

"But I'll tell you what," he continued, "I'll give them a call just to make sure, okay?"

Sam nodded and smiled for the first time since he'd walked into the Fish and Game building. As the officer dialed the phone, Sam squeezed his eyes shut and crossed his fingers as hard as he could.

The officer walked into another room and talked to the zoo for an awfully long time. Sam strained to listen, but he couldn't hear a thing.

When the officer hung up the phone he looked at Sam and shook his head.

What-what-what??? thought Sam.

"It looks like you're in luck," the officer said with a grin. "It seems the zoo just shipped three young otters to a marine park in Chicago, so they have room for your baby ..."

"Yahoo!" cried Sam, dancing around the office, hugging the otter tightly to his chest.

" . . . but hold on. They *also* said that there's a good chance your otter won't make it through the night. He hasn't been fed for at least 24 hours and he may be too weak to survive."

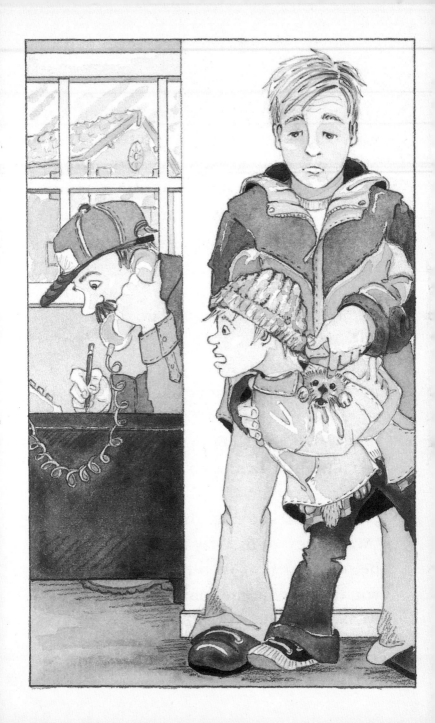

"Oh, he'll survive," said Sam with a grin. "This is one tough little otter."

"I hope so. If he's still alive in the morning, they'll send someone to pick him up. They said I could try feeding him through the night, but he may not accept food from a bottle."

"But you've got to let *me* take him home," pleaded Sam. "He doesn't even know you."

Dad shook his head. "Sam, this is not a pet. You've got to understand that."

"I DO understand," replied Sam, "But he's scared. I've GOT to stay with him. I'll . . . I'll just stay here with you tonight," Sam said to the officer.

To Sam's surprise, the officer smiled. "Well, they didn't say I couldn't get a helper. I guess it won't hurt anything if you take him home tonight."

"Yeaaahhhh!" roared Sam.

Waa-aaa-aaa! wailed the hungry otter.

Dad just rolled his eyes and sighed. "What do we feed him?" Dad asked the officer.

"The zoo suggested you blend up herring, cream, and cod liver oil, and put it in a baby bottle."

Gross! thought Sam.

Dad and Sam stopped at the general store to buy the cream and a baby bottle. They went to the cannery to get the herring. And at the drug store they bought cod liver oil. The pharmacist smiled at Sam, "This'll put hair on your chest."

"Oh, it's not for me!" Sam assured him. "It's for my otter."

They left the pharmacist scratching his head.

"Phew! What's that smell?" exclaimed Mom, when they finally got home.

"Look, Mom!" said Sam, drawing the

baby otter from his jacket.

"Oh, how wonderful!" cried Mom. "Where in the world did you find him?"

While Sam told her the story, she held the baby otter and stroked his fur. He wasn't squirming anymore, and even worse, he wasn't crying either.

Dad put two herring in the blender, then added half the cod liver oil and half the cream. *WHHRRRR!* The mix looked—well—pretty awful. And the smell! They all plugged their noses.

Dad snipped a hole in the nipple so the thick, sludgy goo could flow out. He filled the baby bottle with the mix and handed Mom the bottle.

"Here goes nothing," Mom said, putting the nipple against the otter's mouth. But he wouldn't eat.

"Looks like the otter's not hungry," said Dad. "This may not work after all."

7

A Long (and Smelly) Night

Can I try, Mom?" asked Sam.
"Why not?" she said, handing him the quiet otter and the bottle.

"Maybe if I squeeze a little out first he'll get the idea," Sam said, squeezing the bottle until some goo came out. The baby otter licked its mouth. Sam squeezed out a little more. The otter licked again.

"He's eating!" Mom and Dad cried at the same time.

Waaa-waaa. Waaa-waaa, whined the little otter as if to say, "Quit talking and keep squeezing!"

"It looks like you've got a long night ahead of you, Sam," said Dad. "My guess is he's going to want to eat every few minutes."

"No problem," crowed Sam, with a huge grin.

Sam made a bed for them on a blanket in front of the woodstove. He looked longingly at the couch, but Mom had been firm: no sea otters on the furniture!

Sure enough, the little otter mewed constantly, demanding to be fed. After a few hours, Sam got a big cramp in his arm. At midnight, the otter finally quieted down.

Sam curled up with the otter on his chest and they both fell sound asleep. But just as Sam was starting to dream ...

Waaa-waaa, the otter whined right in Sam's face. Its fishy breath filled Sam's nose and mouth.

Sam forced his eyes open. "Not again!"

He stumbled to the kitchen to refill the bottle of goo. The kitchen clock said 1:20 A.M. *How can such a little otter hold all that food?* wondered Sam. *You'd think he'd have to go to the bathroom by now ... UH OH!*

Sam raced back into the living room. Sure enough, there was a huge puddle of—YUCK!—otter poop on the blanket!

Waaa-waaa. Waaa-waaa, cried the little otter.

Sam pushed the dirty blanket aside and fed the baby until it fell asleep again. Then he mopped up the mess with a great many paper towels. Then he put the blanket in the washing machine. Finally, he lay down and fell instantly to sleep.

Before he knew it, Sam heard the familiar *waaa-aa, waaa-aa*. He shuffled into the kitchen. Four o'clock in the morning!

Sam put the last of the goo into the bottle. He was so sleepy that he didn't notice the tiny puddle of goo on the kitchen floor. It turned out to be ...

Incredibly ...

Awfully ...

SLIPPERY!

Zoom! went Sam's feet, sailing into the air.

Bamm! went his body, hitting the floor.

Slam! went the bottle, skidding across the room.

Luckily, neither Sam nor the bottle was broken. He picked it up and fed the last of the sludge to the hungry otter. Sam was very tired. But finally, so was the otter.

This time they both snored away until daylight.

"Peeyew! What's that smell?" Mom asked, wrinkling her nose as she came down for breakfast.

"Otter poop," said Sam, with a yawn.

"Powerful stuff," laughed Mom.

"How's the baby?" asked Dad.

"I think he's going to make it," replied Sam. "He polished off two and a half bottles last night!"

Dad called the Fish and Game officer and reported Sam's success. "The zoo is sending someone to pick up the otter," reported Dad. "I'm picking her up at the airport in two hours."

Sam nodded. Despite the troublesome night, he had fallen in love with the little otter.

Mom put an arm around Sam's shoulders. "I know it'll be tough to give him up, honey, but you have to remember that he belongs with other otters, not with us. He'll be happier at the zoo."

But Sam wasn't listening. He was wondering if the otter could live at Sandy Beach instead. Maybe he could finish his fort and stay there and take care of the otter for the summer ...

8

Saying Good-bye

The morning flew by. Sam fed the little otter and it napped in his arms. He stroked its fuzzy head. Before he knew it, Dad was off to the airport.

Sam hoped maybe the zoo lady had missed her plane. Or maybe the plane had broken down so she couldn't fly. Or maybe an elephant caught a cold and she had to stay in Anchorage.

When he heard the pickup truck pull into the driveway and two doors slam, Sam's heart sank.

Shoot! She was here. He hadn't yet

figured out how he was going to convince her to let him keep the otter in his fort at Sandy Beach!

As they came into the house, Dad called, "Sam, come meet Miss O'Brien."

Reluctantly, Sam walked into the kitchen. "Hi," he mumbled, without looking up.

A hand reached down to shake his and he lifted his head to look into the nicest face he had ever seen. Miss O'Brien sure was pretty for a zoo lady, and she was giving him a big smile.

Sam smiled back in spite of himself.

"It's a real honor to meet you, Sam."

Me?? An HONOR? thought Sam. *Wow!*

"Not many people have been able to keep a baby sea otter alive, especially after it has been abandoned and is starving. You must have spent a long night working hard."

"You can say that again," said Sam through a mouth-stretching yawn.

Miss O'Brien laughed and continued, "I want you to know, Sam, that we'll take the very best care of your little otter. He'll have a huge pool to swim in and lots of other otters to play with.

"And," she added, "no eagles to bother him!"

That didn't sound too bad to Sam, but he still had his plan. "I don't see why he can't stay here with us," said Sam, "I could raise him in my fort at Sandy Beach and teach him everything. I could turn him loose in the bay when he got big enough to catch his own food."

Miss O'Brien smiled her big smile again. "Oh Sam, I wish you could do just that. I know you'd be a very good caretaker. But there are just too many problems with keeping him here."

"Like what?" asked Sam, stubbornly. He wasn't going to give in, no matter how much Miss O'Brien smiled.

"For one thing, you have a dog, don't you?"

"Yes," replied Sam, "Her name is Neptune, and she's very gentle. She wouldn't hurt anything."

"I'm sure that's true, Sam. I'll bet you've trained her well. But did you know that sea otters can catch diseases from dogs? Your otter could get so sick he could die."

"Oh," said Sam, looking at Neptune.

"Also, if you turned your little otter loose in the bay, he might get in the way of a boat, and be hurt. Unlike a wild sea otter, he wouldn't know that boats are dangerous."

Sam thought about the hundreds of boats that roared in and out of the harbor all summer. He shuddered.

"Sam, why don't you show Miss O'Brien the otter?" suggested Dad.

Sam led Miss O'Brien to the nest of blankets. Sam had helped with mopping the floor and washing the blankets to make a new bed. The little otter was curled up on Sam's pillow.

"He's beautiful, Sam."

Miss O'Brien picked up the baby and held him next to Sam's cheek so he could say good-bye. Despite his resolve, Sam felt hot tears rolling down his cheeks. He couldn't stop them, so he turned and ran upstairs.

From his bed, Sam could hear the engine of Dad's pickup truck starting and then they were gone. So was his baby sea otter.

9

Sadness and Surprises

Sam was so sad that he couldn't eat. That night, he just picked at his dinner. On Monday, he dragged himself to school and sat by himself at lunch. He sulked all week, even refusing offers from the older boys to play kickball after school in the spring sunshine.

"Hey Sam. We need a second baseman. Come on!" urged Billy Sutton.

"No thanks," said Sam.

"Okay, you can play first base, Sam," said Darwin Chambers. He was Melody's cousin and as nice as Melody was bossy.

Normally, Sam would have jumped at the chance to play with the older boys, but today he just didn't have the heart. He also couldn't tell them why. He was afraid that if he tried to explain about his baby otter, he'd burst into tears. Then they'd never ever ask him to do anything again.

"I've got to help my Dad on the boat," said Sam. It was a lie, but it made sense. Their fathers were fishermen too.

"Maybe another day then," said Billy.

"Yeah, maybe," mumbled Sam.

By Thursday, Sam was still in a funk. Mom and Dad came into his room and sat on the bed.

"Sam, we need to go to Anchorage this weekend for supplies. Would you like to go with us?"

Sam perked up. "Yeah! Can we leave tomorrow morning?"

"I'm afraid not, son," laughed Dad, "You have school tomorrow. We'll leave on the ferry tomorrow afternoon."

Sam could hardly sit through school on Friday. This time, when he turned down after-school invitations from Billy and Darwin, it was with a happy smile.

"I'm going to Anchorage!"

"Man, you're so lucky," said Darwin. "You'll probably get to see the new movies and go to the mall and eat pizza till you bust."

And maybe go to the zoo, thought Sam.

On the ferry, Sam hung over the rail and waved at the sea otters floating in the

kelp beds. He hoped they'd have time to see his otter soon.

In the truck, Sam slept during the long drive. He hardly noticed when Dad pulled into a motel and carried him into the room.

Saturday was warm and sunny. The trees in the city showed signs of new leaves. Sam woke with the sun in his face.

The motel clock said 7:10.

"Okay, let's get the errands done," he announced.

"Oh, Sam, we have a long list and then a long drive back to Homer. You'll have to relax," said Mom.

But Sam couldn't relax. He fidgeted through breakfast. He bounced up and down on the truck seat and raced up and down the aisles at the grocery store. He jumped on and off the stacks of lumber at the lumberyard, and tied knots in the big coils of rope at the marine supply store.

Finally, it was noon.

"Are we done yet?" urged Sam.

"Not yet!" said his weary parents. "We have one last errand to run before we go."

They couldn't leave Anchorage without going to the zoo! What more could they possibly need to do? thought Sam in dismay. This was the worst trip he'd ever had!

10

The Sea Otter Gets a Name

Dad turned the truck south and headed away from the city.

"Where are we going?" asked Sam.

"One last errand," replied Dad mysteriously.

Dad winked and then Sam knew—they WERE going to the zoo! Finally!

At the zoo, Sam ran through the gate, past the black bear cage and the wolverines, past the lynx and the caribou, past the sea lion tank, and skidded to a stop in front of the sea otter exhibit.

There was Miss O'Brien giving directions

to a man who was mixing food in a bucket. She gave Sam a big smile.

"Hello, Sam. We've been expecting you."

"You have?" asked Sam. He looked at his smiling parents. They had planned this all along!

"Come look at your baby," said Miss O'Brien, leading him to the far end of the sea otter pen. Sam pressed his face against the glass. He wished he could go inside but Miss O'Brien explained that adult sea otters can bite—hard—if they are scared. Thinking about how sharp the baby's teeth were when he nipped, Sam understood.

"Wow!" exclaimed Sam. It had only been one week, but the little otter had sure grown! He was practically twice as big as before. He didn't look like such a helpless baby anymore.

A big otter swam over to the baby and pulled him onto her chest.

"That female has adopted him, Sam. Her baby got sick and died about ten days ago, and now she's taken over caring for your baby. This is very unusual behavior, but we're thrilled."

Sam watched as the big otter groomed the little baby. Over and over she stroked and fluffed his fur.

"She's fluffing up his fur with air so he stays warm and dry," explained Miss O'Brien. "That's an important part of caring for a sea otter."

Sam watched the otters swim, and play, and dive, and feed. He watched them groom their fur, and roll over and over in the water. Some of them slept on their backs, their faces turned to the sun, their paws held together under their chins.

Sam especially watched the baby. He was a bit disappointed that it didn't seem to notice him.

All too soon it was time to go.

"We'll come back again this summer, Sam, so you can see how your baby has grown," said Dad, putting his arm around Sam's shoulders.

Sam nodded. He didn't feel as sad now that the baby otter had a mom to take care of it. He smiled at his own mom as she ruffled his hair.

"Sam, wait!" called Miss O'Brien. "There's one more thing I want to show you."

She led him to the front of the sea otter exhibit. On one wall of the tank were signs that told about each otter and listed the name the zoo people had given them. There was "Grumpy" and "Whiskers" and and ... hey, there was a brand new sign!

The Anchorage Zoo is pleased to welcome a new sea otter to our exhibit. The baby otter was found abandoned near Seldovia by a young boy named Sam Peterson. The 8-year-old boy nursed the starving baby otter until it could be transported to the zoo. In recognition of Sam Peterson, we have named the new otter "SAM."

Sam looked back at his baby otter. It was on its new mother's tummy, but she had paddled close to the glass. The little otter was looking right at him!

Waaa-aa, Waaa-aa, it cried.

Sam grinned at Miss O'Brien.

"So what do you think, is that a good name for your otter?" she asked him.

"It's perfect," Sam replied. "Just perfect."